Chinese Legends

Three Popular Stories

The Legend of the Chinese Zodiac Animals
The Legend of Chang Er & Mid-Autumn Festival
The Legend of Qu Yuan & Duan Wu Festival

Bilingual

English & Simplified Chinese with Pinyin

Audio book available on our website www.superspeakjuniors.com. Alternatively, scan the QR code on the back cover. Audio book available in English, Cantonese and Mandarin.

This book is printed in English and Simplified Chinese with Pinyin (Pinyin is a standard phonetic system for writing Mandarin using Roman letters.)

Our Other Books

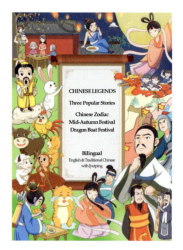

**Chinese Legends
Three Popular Stories**
Bilingual Edition—
English &
Traditional Chinese
with Jyutping

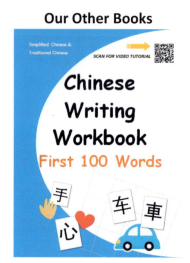

**Chinese Writing Workbook
First 100 Words**
Simplified & Traditional Chinese
with Pinyin & Jyutping

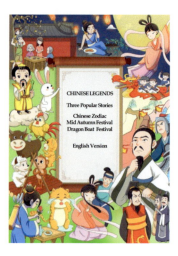

**Chinese Legends
Three Popular Stories**
English Edition

Published by Super Speak Juniors
ISBN 978-1-8381799-1-5
All rights reserved. No part of this publication may be reproduced, stored or transmitted in any form or by any means, electronic, photocopying, recording or otherwise, without the prior written permission of the Publisher.
Story retold and translated by M Kan and H Wang.

For Ben, Max & Yutao

CONTENTS

1. The Legend of the Chinese Zodiac Animals
2. The Legend of Chang Er & Mid-Autumn Festival
3. The Legend of Qu Yuan & Duan Wu Festival

The Legend of the Chinese Zodiac Animals

A long, long time ago, in ancient China, people did not know how to measure months and years. They went to seek help from the Heavenly Jade Emperor. The Jade Emperor thought naming the years after animals would help people to remember them. However, with so many animals in the world, which twelve should he choose?

很久很久以前,在古代的中国,人们不知道如何度量月份和年份。他们找到玉皇大帝寻求帮助。玉皇大帝想通过以动物的名字来命名年份,这样容易让人们记住。但是,世界上这么多种动物,选择哪十二个动物呢?

"I know!" said the Jade Emperor. "I will hold a competition on my birthday! The first twelve animals to cross the river will earn a place on the Chinese zodiac." When the news of the race was announced, all the animals were very excited.

wǒ zhī dào le　　yù huáng dà dì shuō　　wǒ jiāng zài wǒ shēng rì de nà tiān jǔ bàn yī

"我 知 道 了!" 玉 皇 大 帝 说。"我 将 在 我 生 日 的 那 天 举 办 一

cì bǐ sài　qián shí èr gè tōng guò hé liú de dòng wù jiāng chéng wéi shí èr shēng xiào de

次 比 赛! 前 十 二 个 通 过 河 流 的 动 物 将 成 为 十 二 生 肖 的

yī yuán　　dāng bǐ sài de xiāo xī gōng bù hòu　suǒ yǒu de dòng wù dōu fēi cháng jī dòng

一 员。" 当 比 赛 的 消 息 公 布 后, 所 有 的 动 物 都 非 常 激 动。

The cat and the rat used to be best friends. The night before the race, the rat said to his dear friend cat, "I really want to have a year named after me, but there is no way I will make it across the river because I cannot swim."

猫和老鼠是非常好的朋友。比赛前的晚上,老鼠跟猫说:"我真的很想有一年以我的名字命名,但是我肯定赢不了,因为我不会游泳。"

"Don't worry," said the cat, "since we cannot swim, we should ask for help. We can ask the ox to help us across."

bié dān xīn　　　māo shuō　 jì rán wǒ mén bú huì yóu yǒng, wǒ mén jiù děi zhǎo qí tā
"别 担 心," 猫 说,"既 然 我 们 不 会 游 泳,我 们 就 得 找 其 他
dòng wù bāng máng　 wǒ mén kě yǐ jiào niú dài wǒ mén guò qù
动 物 帮 忙。 我 们 可 以 叫 牛 带 我 们 过 去。"

The day of the Jade Emperor's birthday and the important race had arrived! The kind ox agreed to help the rat and the cat. "Climb on to my back!" he said.

玉皇大帝生日和重要比赛的日子终于到了!好心的牛同意帮助猫和老鼠。"爬到我的背上吧!"他说。

The rat and the cat happily sat on the ox's back. Then the ox started to swim across. As the rat lay comfortably on the ox's back, he began to wonder how to gain first place.

老鼠和猫高兴地坐在牛的背上,然后牛就开始游出去。当老鼠舒服地躺在牛背上时,他开始想如何夺得第一名。

He suddenly thought of an evil plan. He turned to the cat and when the cat wasn't looking, the sneaky rat pushed the cat into the river! "Splash!"

tū rán, tā xiǎng dào yī gè xié è de jì huà. tā nuó dào māo páng biān, dāng māo méi yǒu zhù yì de shí hòu, jiǎo huá de lǎo shǔ bǎ māo tuī xià hé! pā

突然,他想到一个邪恶的计划。他挪到猫旁边,当猫没有注意的时候,狡猾的老鼠把猫推下河!"啪!"

The rat then hopped up to the ox's head and hid in his ear. The ox turned his head to look back and thought both the cat and the rat had fallen into the river. He couldn't save them so he carried on with his race.

rán hòu lǎo shǔ cuàn dào niú de tóu shàng cáng zài tā de ěr duǒ lǐ niú zhuǎn tóu wǎng hòu
然后老鼠窜到牛的头上,藏在他的耳朵里。牛转头往后
kàn yǐ wéi māo hé lǎo shǔ dōu diào jìn hé lǐ le tā jiù bù liǎo tā men yú shì
看,以为猫和老鼠都掉进河里了。他救不了他们,于是
tā jì xù bǐ sài
他继续比赛。

When the ox approached the river bank, he was very excited as he thought he was about to win. Then suddenly, the cunning rat jumped out of his ear and bolted forward like a flash of lightning. The sneaky rat ran past the finish line to win first place!

当牛接近河岸的时候,他非常激动以为他要赢了。突然,狡猾的老鼠跳出他的耳朵,像闪电一样冲向前。狡猾的老鼠跑过终点取得了第一名。

The Jade Emperor was very surprised to see the rat was the first to arrive. "Little rat," he said, "you cannot swim, how did you win the race?" The sneaky rat proudly replied, "I cannot swim, but I am clever!"

玉皇大帝很惊讶看到老鼠第一个到达。"小老鼠,"他说,"你不会游泳,是怎么赢得比赛的?"狡猾的老鼠自豪地答道:"我虽然不会游泳,但是我聪明!"

Just then, the angry ox arrived. He was very unhappy the rat had tricked him. The Jade Emperor awarded the hard-working ox with second place.

jiù zài nà shí qì hū hū de niú dào dá le tā fēi cháng bù gāo xìng lǎo shǔ shuǎ le
就在那时,气呼呼的牛到达了。他非常不高兴老鼠耍了
tā yù huáng dà dì shòu yǔ qín fèn de niú wéi dì èr míng
他。玉皇大帝授予勤奋的牛为第二名。

A little while later, the tiger arrived. The tiger had used all his strength to swim across the river. The Jade Emperor was impressed with his hard work and said, "The third year of the zodiac will be named after you!"

guò le yī huì er lǎo hǔ dào dá le lǎo hǔ yòng jìn le tā quán bù de lì qì yóu
过了一会儿，老虎到达了。老虎用尽了他全部的力气游
guò hé yù huáng dà dì duì tā de nǔ lì yìn xiàng shēn kè bìng shuō dì sān nián de
过河。玉皇大帝对他的努力印象深刻，并说："第三年的
shēng xiào jiāng yǐ nǐ de míng zì mìng míng
生肖将以你的名字命名。"

Suddenly, there was a strong gust of wind. Out hopped a rabbit to win fourth place. The rabbit said, "I cannot swim, but I can hop. I used items in the river as stepping stones to cross the river!"

突然,一阵强风吹过。兔子跳出来赢得第四名。兔子说:"我不会游泳,但我会跳。我利用河里的物体作为落脚点通过了河流。"

The next to arrive was the flying dragon. The Jade Emperor said, "You can fly, so I expected you to win first place. Why did you arrive so late?" The dragon replied, "On my way to the race, I went to make rain for a village." According to legend, the dragon was responsible for creating rain. The dragon continued, "On my flight over the river, I saw a rabbit struggle to cross the river, so I blew him to the river bank."

下一个到达的是会飞的龙。玉皇大帝说:"你能飞,我以为你会赢得第一名。为什么你到得这么晚?"龙回答:"我在比赛的途中去了给村庄降雨。"传说中龙是负责降雨的。龙又继续说:"当我飞过河流时,我看到兔子正在拼命挣扎着过河,于是我把他吹到河岸上。"

Just then, they heard the sound of a galloping horse. "It's horse!" exclaimed the Jade Emperor. "He will get sixth place!"

正当那时,他们听到飞驰的马蹄声。"是马!"玉皇大帝大声说道,"他将是第六名。"

But before the horse crossed the finish line, a snake that was coiled around the horse's hoof slithered out. Startled, the horse sprang back. "Thank you for bringing me here," hissed the crafty snake as he slithered across the finish line to win sixth place.

但是就在马穿过终点前一刻,一条卷在马蹄上的蛇爬了出来。马吓得往后跳了一下。"谢谢你带我过来!"狡猾的蛇爬过终点夺得第六名。

"Well, that was a surprise!" laughed the Jade Emperor as he awarded the horse with seventh place.

èn nà zhēn yì wài yù huáng dà dì xiào zhe shòu yǔ mǎ wéi dì qī míng
"嗯,那真意外!"玉皇大帝笑着授予马为第七名。

Shortly after, they saw the goat, the monkey and the rooster reach the river bank on a raft. "Why did you come together?" asked Jade Emperor curiously.

过了一会儿,大家看到羊,猴子和公鸡撑着木筏到达河岸。"你们为什么会一起到达?"玉皇大帝好奇地问道。

"When the race started, we saw a piece of wood nearby. We all climbed on to it and helped one another across!" the three animals chimed. The Jade Emperor was impressed with their team work and happily awarded the goat eighth place, the monkey ninth place and the rooster tenth place.

"比赛开始的时候,我们看到一根木头在附近,我们一起爬上去,然后互相合作通过了河流。"那三只动物附和着说。玉皇大帝对他们团体合作印象深刻,高兴地授予羊为第八名,猴子为第九名,公鸡为第十名。

"Woof! Woof!" two barks came from the finish line. The dog had arrived! The dog was a good swimmer but he wasted time playing in the water, so he only got eleventh place.

"汪！汪！"两声狗叫从终点线传过来。狗到了！狗是个游泳好手,但是他忙着玩水浪费了很多时间,因此,他只能取得第十一名。

"Which animal will be the last member of the zodiac?" wondered the Jade Emperor. Just then, the pig arrived. The Jade Emperor awarded the pig with the last place in the zodiac.

"哪个动物会成为十二生肖的最后一员呢?" 玉皇大帝想。就在那时,猪到达了。玉皇大帝授予猪为十二生肖的最后一名成员。

Finally, the cat arrived, his body dripping with water. He was extremely upset he did not make it into the top twelve and he would never forget who pushed him into the river. From that day onwards, the cat and the rat became mortal enemies.

终于,猫到达了,身上湿淋淋地滴着水。他非常伤心没能进入前十二名,同时他永远不会忘记是谁把他推进河里。自从那天以后,猫和老鼠就成为了永远的敌人。

The Legend of Chang Er & Mid-Autumn Festival

A long, long time ago, in ancient China, there were ten suns in the sky. "It's too hot!" people cried. The heat from the suns scorched all the crops and made the lives of people and animals a misery.

很久很久以前,在古代的中国,天上有十个太阳。"太热了!"人们喊到。太阳的热浪烤焦了所有的庄稼,让人们和动物都活在痛苦中。

One day, a skilled archer named Hou Yi used his bow and arrows to shoot down nine of the suns.

一天，有一个叫后羿的弓箭手，用他的弓和箭射下了九个太阳。

The earth was saved! Hou Yi became a hero and many people rushed to learn archery from him.

地球得救了！后羿成为了英雄，很多人都拜他为师，向他学习射箭。

The Queen of Heaven rewarded Hou Yi with a pill of immortality for his bravery. "This is the pill of immortality. Once you swallow it, you will ascend to heaven and become a god!" she said.

因为后羿的勇敢,西王母赐给他长生不老药。"这是长生不老药丸,一旦吃下去,你就能飞升上天成为神仙。"她说。

Hou Yi wanted to become immortal, but he had a wonderful wife named Chang Er who he loved very much. He could not bear to leave her, so he left the pill of immortality at home.

后羿想长生不老,但是他有一个很好的妻子-嫦娥。他非常爱她,不舍得离开她。于是他把长生不老药留在家里。

One day, one of Hou Yi's naughty students called Pang Meng, sneaked into Hou Yi's house to steal the pill of immortality. Chang Er stumbled upon his despicable act and screamed "No!" To stop the greedy Pang Meng and to protect the pill of immortality, Chang Er swallowed it.

有一天，一个叫逄蒙的弟子心怀不轨，偷偷溜进后羿的家里偷长生不老药。嫦娥发现了他的不轨行为，尖叫道："不要！"为了阻止贪心的逄蒙和保护长生不老药，嫦娥把它吃了。

Chang Er immediately floated up towards the heavens and she stopped at the moon so she could be closer to Earth, where Hou Yi lived.

cháng é lì kè fēi shēng shàng le tiān tā tíng liú zài yuè liàng shàng yīn wèi néng lí hòu yì
嫦娥立刻飞升上了天,她停留在月亮上,因为能离后羿
zhù de dì qiú jìn yī diǎn
住的地球近一点。

Hou Yi missed his wife very much and in memory of Chang Er, he worshipped the moon with different offerings.

hòu yì fēi cháng huái niàn tā de qī zǐ wèi le jì niàn tā tā yòng gè zhǒng fāng shì jì
后 羿 非 常 怀 念 他 的 妻 子，为 了 纪 念 她，他 用 各 种 方 式 祭
bài yuè liàng
拜 月 亮。

Hou Yi hoped to be reunited with Chang Er one day and presented moon cakes as an offering on the fifteenth day of the eighth lunar month every year.

<small>hòu yì xī wàng yǒu yī tiān néng hé cháng é tuán jù tā zài měi nián de nóng lì bā yuè</small>
后羿希望有一天能和嫦娥团聚,他在每年的农历八月
<small>shí wǔ zhè yī tiān yòng yuè bǐng jì sì yuè liàng</small>
十五这一天,用月饼祭祀月亮。

Today, many people in the world celebrate Mid-Autumn Festival on the fifteenth day of the eighth lunar month by uniting with family, eating moon cakes, lighting lanterns and admiring the full moon.

jīn tiān　shì jiè shàng hěn duō rén zài bā yuè shí wǔ zhōng qiū jié zhè yī tiān　yǔ jiā tíng
今天, 世界上很多人在八月十五中秋节这一天, 与家庭
tuán jù　chī yuè bǐng　diǎn dēng lóng hé shǎng yuè
团聚, 吃月饼, 点灯笼和赏月。

The Legend of Qu Yuan & Duan Wu Festival

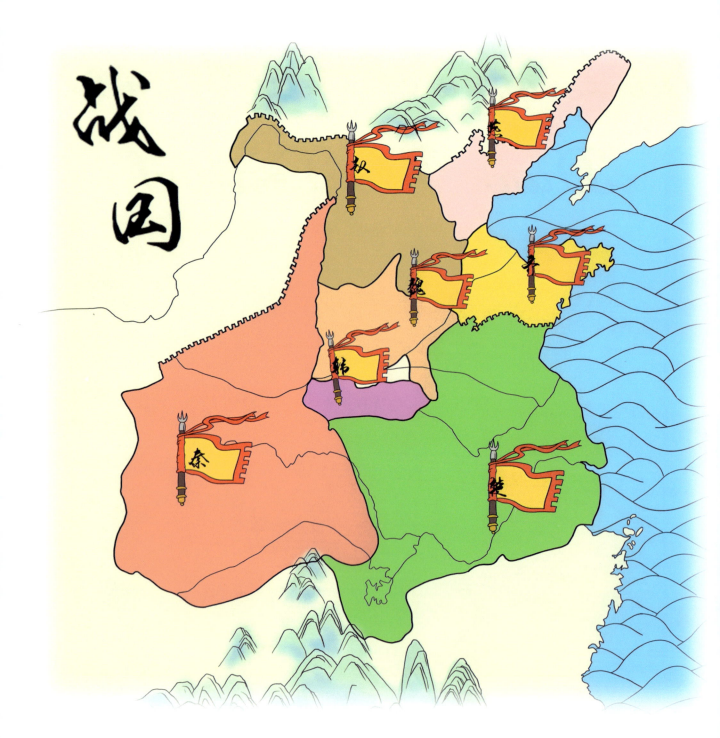

A long, long time ago, China was split into seven kingdoms. They were the Qin, Qi, Chu, Yan, Han, Zhao and Wei kingdoms.

很久很久以前,中国被分为七个国家。它们是秦,齐,楚,燕,韩,赵和魏国。

The seven kingdoms were at war and the Kingdom of Qin was the most powerful. The ruthless King of Qin wanted to rule the whole of China.

这七个国家互相攻伐,而秦国是里面最强大的。无情的秦王想统一整个中国。

In the Kingdom of Chu lived a man called Qu Yuan. Qu Yuan was an educated poet and politician, who was patriotic and dreamed of peace. He was trusted by the King of Chu and loved by the people.

有一个生活在楚国的人叫作屈原。屈原是一名诗人和政治家,他非常热爱楚国和热爱和平,同时也深得楚王的信任和人民的爱戴。

But the King of Chu's confidence in Qu Yuan led to the jealousy of other ministers. They plotted against Qu Yuan and told the King of Chu, "Qu Yuan is a traitor!"

dàn shì chǔ wáng duì qū yuán de xìn rèn zhāo zhì le qí tā dà chén guì zú de jí dù
但是楚王对屈原的信任招致了其他大臣贵族的嫉妒。
tā men mì móu zhēn duì qū yuán xiàng chǔ wáng gào fā qū yuán shì pàn guó zéi
他们密谋针对屈原,向楚王告发:"屈原是叛国贼!"

Sadly, the King of Chu believed the ministers' lies and banished poor Qu Yuan into exile.

bú xìng de shì chǔ wáng xiāng xìn le dà chén mén de huǎng yán bìng bǎ kě lián de qū yuán
不 幸 的 是, 楚 王 相 信 了 大 臣 们 的 谎 言 并 把 可 怜 的 屈 原
liú fàng dào piān pì zhī dì
流 放 到 偏 僻 之 地。

The King of Chu continued to battle with the Kingdom of Qin, but he was eventually beaten by the mighty Qin army.

楚王继续着和秦国的战争,但是他最终还是败给了强大的秦军。

Qu Yuan was heartbroken when he heard the news that his beloved kingdom had been invaded. He jumped into the Miluo river.

屈原听到他挚爱的国家被攻破的消息,非常伤心,跳进了汨罗江。

The people in the Kingdom of Chu were deeply saddened. To stop the fish from feasting on Qu Yuan, they threw parcels of rice wrapped in bamboo leaves into the river to feed the fish. Others banged drums to scare away the fish.

楚国的老百姓非常伤心，为了阻止鱼儿吃掉屈原，他们用竹叶包裹的米饭团投入江中来喂鱼。另外一些人则击鼓把鱼儿吓跑。

To this day, many people remember Qu Yuan by celebrating the Dragon Boat Festival, also called Duan Wu Festival. On the 5th day of the 5th lunar month, people enjoy eating sticky rice wrapped in bamboo leaves and have fun cheering at dragon boat races.

直到今天,人们会以龙舟节,也叫端午节来纪念屈原。在农历五月五日这一天,人们会一边吃竹叶包的粽子,一边欢呼着看龙舟比赛。

Questions

According to the legends in this book:

1. Why do cats hate rats?

2. Why do you think there is egg yolk in mooncake?

3. Why do we eat sticky rice wrapped in bamboo leaves?

Answers

1. Cats hate rats because the rat ruthlessly pushed the cat into the river during the big race to win a place in the Chinese Zodiac.

2. Egg yolks are placed in the middle of mooncakes to represent the full moon in the sky on the 15th day of the 8th lunar month. It is to commemorate Chang Er, who flew to the moon after swallowing the pill of immortality.

3. People eat sticky rice wrapped in bamboo leaves on the 5th day of the 5th lunar month to commemorate Qu Yuan, a famous poet and politician, who jumped into the Miluo river. People threw parcels of sticky rice into the river to feed the fish to save Qu Yuan's body.

Printed in France by Amazon
Brétigny-sur-Orge, FR